Put Beginning Readers on the Right Track with
ALL ABOARD READING™

The All Aboard Reading series is especially designed for beginning readers. Written by noted authors and illustrated in full color, these are books that children really want to read—books to excite their imagination, expand their interests, make them laugh, and support their feelings. With fiction and nonfiction stories that are high interest and curriculum-related, All Aboard Reading books offer something for every young reader. And with four different reading levels, the All Aboard Reading series lets you choose which books are most appropriate for your children and their growing abilities.

Picture Readers
Picture Readers have super-simple texts, with many nouns appearing as rebus pictures. At the end of each book are 24 flash cards—on one side is a rebus picture; on the other side is the written-out word.

Station Stop 1
Station Stop 1 books are best for children who have just begun to read. Simple words and big type make these early reading experiences more comfortable. Picture clues help children to figure out the words on the page. Lots of repetition throughout the text helps children to predict the next word or phrase—an essential step in developing word recognition.

Station Stop 2
Station Stop 2 books are written specifically for children who are reading with help. Short sentences make it easier for early readers to understand what they are reading. Simple plots and simple dialogue help children with reading comprehension.

Station Stop 3
Station Stop 3 books are perfect for children who are reading alone. With longer text and harder words, these books appeal to children who have mastered basic reading skills. More complex stories captivate children who are ready for more challenging books.

In addition to All Aboard Reading books, look for All Aboard Math Readers™ (fiction stories that teach math concepts children are learning in school) and All Aboard Science Readers™ (nonfiction books that explore the most fascinating science topics in age-appropriate language).

All Aboard for happy reading!

Text copyright © 2002 by Gail Herman. Illustrations copyright © 2002 by Stacy Peterson.
All rights reserved. Published by Grosset & Dunlap, a division of Penguin Young Readers
Group, 345 Hudson Street, New York, NY 10014. ALL ABOARD READING and GROSSET
& DUNLAP are trademarks of Penguin Group (USA) Inc. Published simultaneously in
Canada. Printed in the U.S.A.

Herman, Gail, 1959–
I've got the back-to-school blues / by Gail Herman ; illustrated by Stacy Peterson.
p. cm. – (All aboard reading)
Summary: When she learns that she will not be in the same class as her friends, Annie worries
about starting second grade with a new teacher.
[1. Schools—Fiction. 2. Teachers—Fiction.] I. Peterson, Stacy, ill. II. Title. III. Series.
PZ7.H4315 Iv 2002
[E]—dc21
                    2002003551

ISBN 0-448-42833-4 (GB)   A B C D E F G H I J
ISBN 0-448-42832-6 (pb)   B C D E F G H I J

All Aboard Reading

Station Stop 2

I've Got the Back-to-School Blues

By Gail Herman

Illustrated by Stacy Peterson

Grosset & Dunlap • New York

When Annie and Katie and
Laura were five,
they were in the same kindergarten class.

When they were six,

they were in the same first-grade class.

But now they were seven.

Katie and Laura were going to be

in the same second-grade class.

But not Annie.

Annie sat on her steps

and looked at her best friends.

They were right next to her,

like they had always been.

But second grade would change everything.

"Tomorrow is the first day of school,"
Annie told her friends.
"You two will be together.
And I'll be with . . . "

Annie got the class list.

Sure, she knew some of the kids.

There was Martin.

He hardly ever spoke.

Then there was Eric.

He was okay.

But he only liked dinosaurs
and baseball.

And there were Sara and Emma.

All they did was play <u>together</u>.

"I'll be with nobody!" Annie said.

"Come on, Annie," said Katie.
"Second grade is not the end
of the world.
Our classroom will be next door."

"That's right," Laura agreed.

"And you can visit.

You know our teacher Mr. Carr.

He likes kids to stop by and say hi."

Sure, Annie knew Mr. Carr.

Everyone wanted him for a teacher.

His class played games, sang songs,

and went on great field trips.

And her teacher?

She was new.

Annie didn't know one thing about her.

TOADY

"What's your teacher's name again?"

Katie asked.

Annie frowned.

Katie knew the teacher's name.

She just wanted to hear it again.

"Ms. Toady," Annie finally said.

Katie and Laura laughed.

Second grade might not be
the end of the world,
Annie thought.
But it sure felt that way.

When Laura and Katie left,

Annie stayed outside.

Maybe if she didn't move,

tomorrow would never come.

School would never start.

"Hey you!" called a girl riding by
on her bike.
It was Jenna,
another second-grader.
Annie hoped she would keep going.
Jenna could be awfully mean.
Screech! Jenna stopped.

"I know you have Ms. Toady,"
Jenna sang in a loud voice.
"Toady, Toady, Toady.
Hopping in the roady."

Jenna laughed.

"I heard she's the meanest teacher ever.

And she's just like her name.

She eats flies.

She has warts.

And she doesn't walk.

She hops."

Screech! Jenna took off.

Annie didn't believe all that frog stuff.

Not really.

But what if Ms. Toady was

the meanest teacher ever?

22

Annie was so upset,

she jumped up to run inside.

All at once, she stopped.

"A moving truck," she said.

A new family was moving in,

just down the block.

There could be someone her age.

Maybe someone in her class.

So when Ms. Toady did something mean,

they could talk about it.

Maybe even laugh about it.

Annie walked closer.

She peered at the furniture

and clothes.

No kids' stuff.

Not even baby things.

Then a woman came out.

She smiled at Annie.

"Hello," she said.

"Hello," said Annie.

"Annie?" her mom called from

the house.

"Where are you?

Dinner is ready."

Annie turned to go. *Meow!*

A cat ran through her legs,

and down the street.

"Oh, no!" the woman cried. "Puffball!"

"I'll get her!" said Annie.

In a flash, she scooped up the cat.

"Here," she told the woman.

"Thank you so much," said the woman.

"Your name is Annie?"

Annie nodded.

"I'm—"

Just then, a second cat ran the other way.

"Sorry! Got to go!" the woman said.

"Annie!" her mom called louder.

"Come in right now!"

Annie waved to the woman.

She seemed nice.

If she had kids,

they would be nice, too.

But all the woman had were cats.

Nothing ever worked out right!

That night, Annie tossed and turned.

She hardly slept at all.

She kept thinking about school.

About second grade

with mean Ms. Toady—

and no friends in class!

At breakfast, Annie tried to eat.

But she had a big lump in her throat.

It was hard to swallow.

Her mom gave her a hug.

"I know you are nervous about school," she said.

"Try not to worry.

You'll make new friends.

And Laura and Katie will still be your best friends."

Annie nodded, but she didn't believe it.

Katie and Laura would talk about
their class.

People she didn't know.

They would walk home—just the two
of them.

Pretty soon, they'd forget all about her.

Annie sighed.

If only she didn't have Ms. Toady!

A little later,

Annie walked into her classroom.

She looked all around.

Emma was talking to Sara.

Max was talking to Martin.

Everyone was talking to somebody.

Everyone but Annie.

All at once, she gasped.

A mean-looking woman bent over a desk.

She had green skin.

Well, almost green skin.

And big bulging eyes.

Well, really big eyes.

Ms. Toady!

The woman stacked some papers.

Then she turned to go.

She was only bringing notices!

She wasn't Ms. Toady after all.

And now Annie could see someone else.

Someone behind that woman.

It was her new neighbor, from down

the block.

The one with the runaway cats.

And she was coming over!

"Hello," the woman said.

"I'm Ms. Toady.

We didn't get to talk the other day.

I'm so glad you are in my class."

"To tell the truth," she went on.

"I feel a little nervous.

After all, I'm new to the neighborhood,

and to school.

Maybe you can help me?

Show me around?"

Annie smiled.

All along, she'd been feeling

sorry for herself.

But poor Ms. Toady.

She must feel really alone.

"Sure," Annie said. "I am happy to help."

After school, Annie walked outside

and grinned.

Katie and Laura were waiting!

They didn't forget her.

"Hi!" Annie said.

Then she saw Ms. Toady.

"Good-bye, Ms. Toady," she called out.

This time, no one laughed.

"Your teacher said hello
to me in the hall," Katie said.
"She seems really nice."
Annie smiled. "She is."

"I'm going to love school this year!"